I Go Up

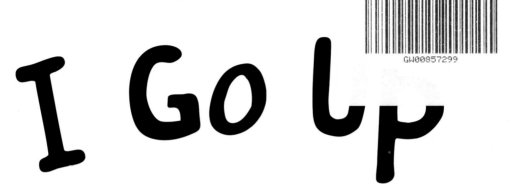

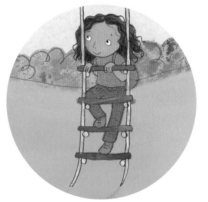

by **Jay Dale**
illustrated by Amanda Gulliver

I go up the stairs.

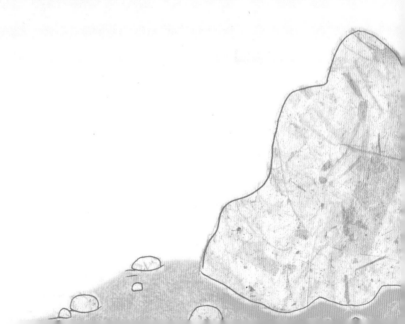

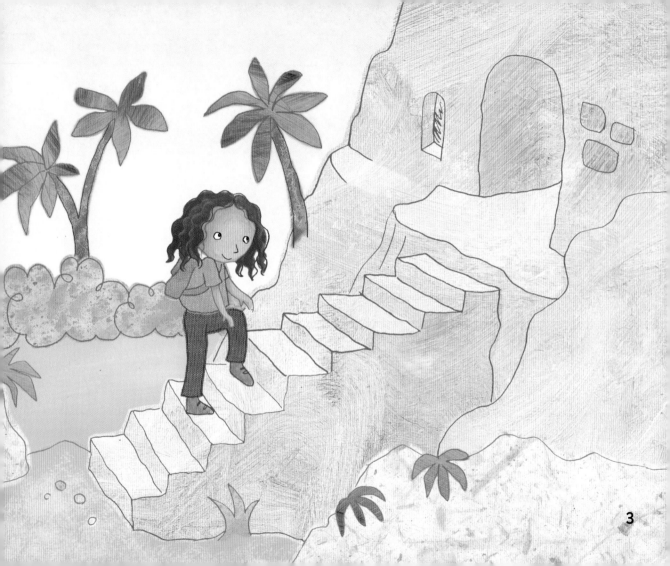

I go up the ladder.

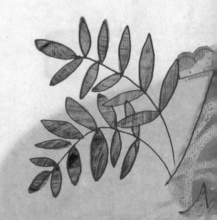

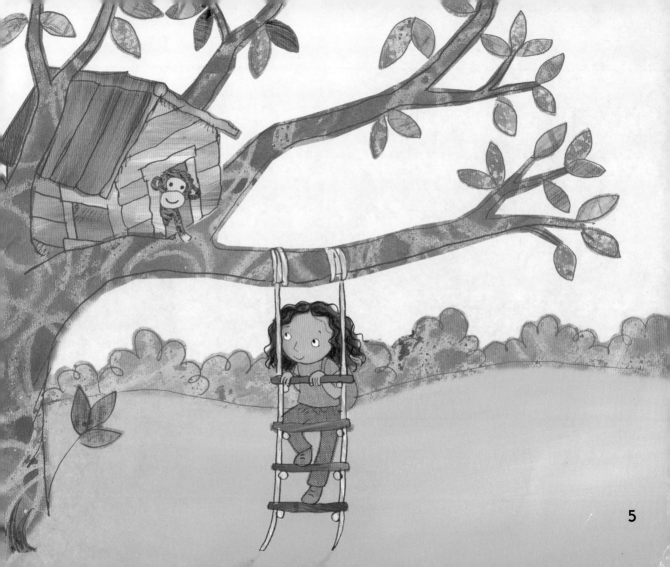

I go up the rope.

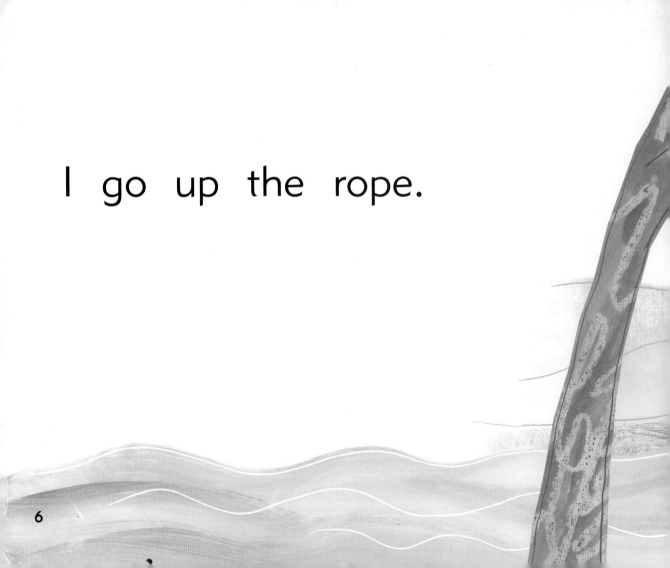

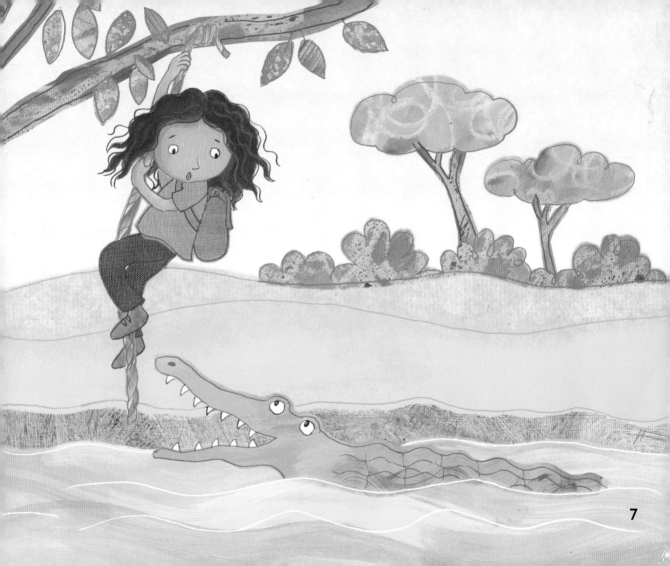

I go up the hill.

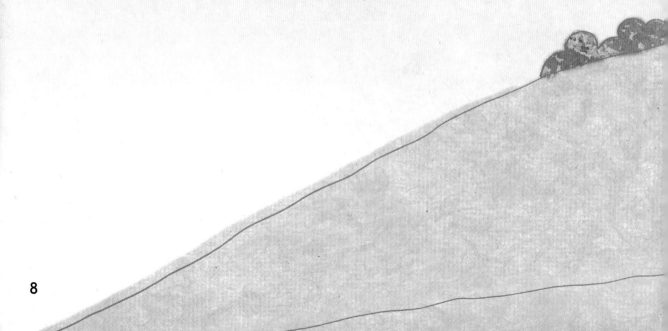

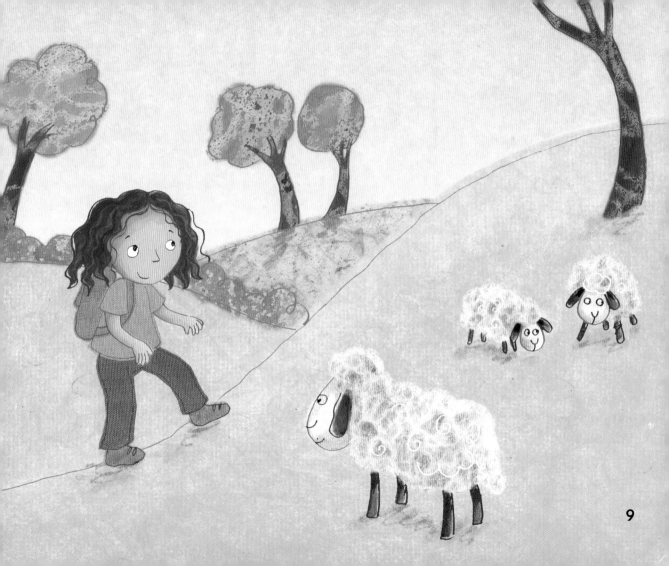

I go up the tree.

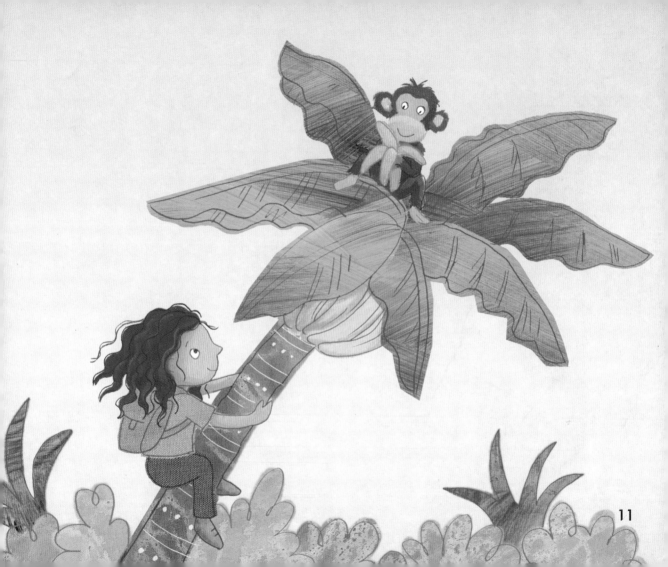

I go up the mountain.

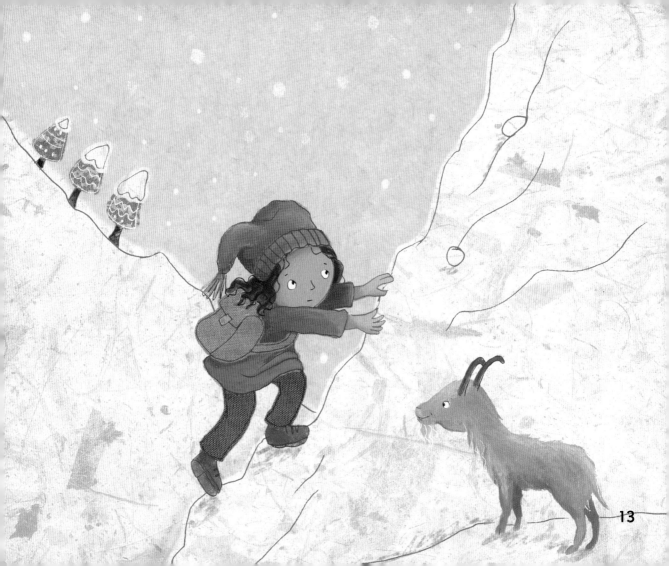

13

I go up...

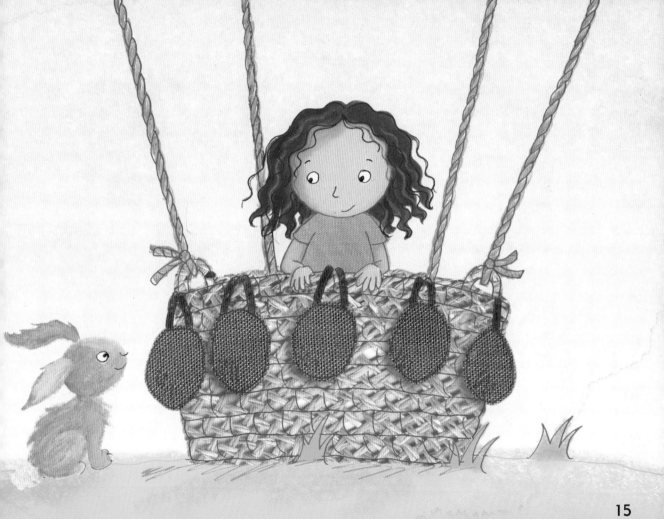

...up, up, up.

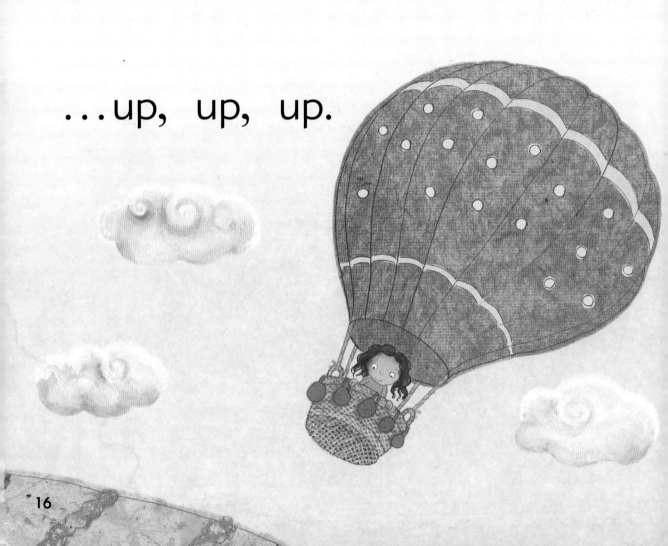